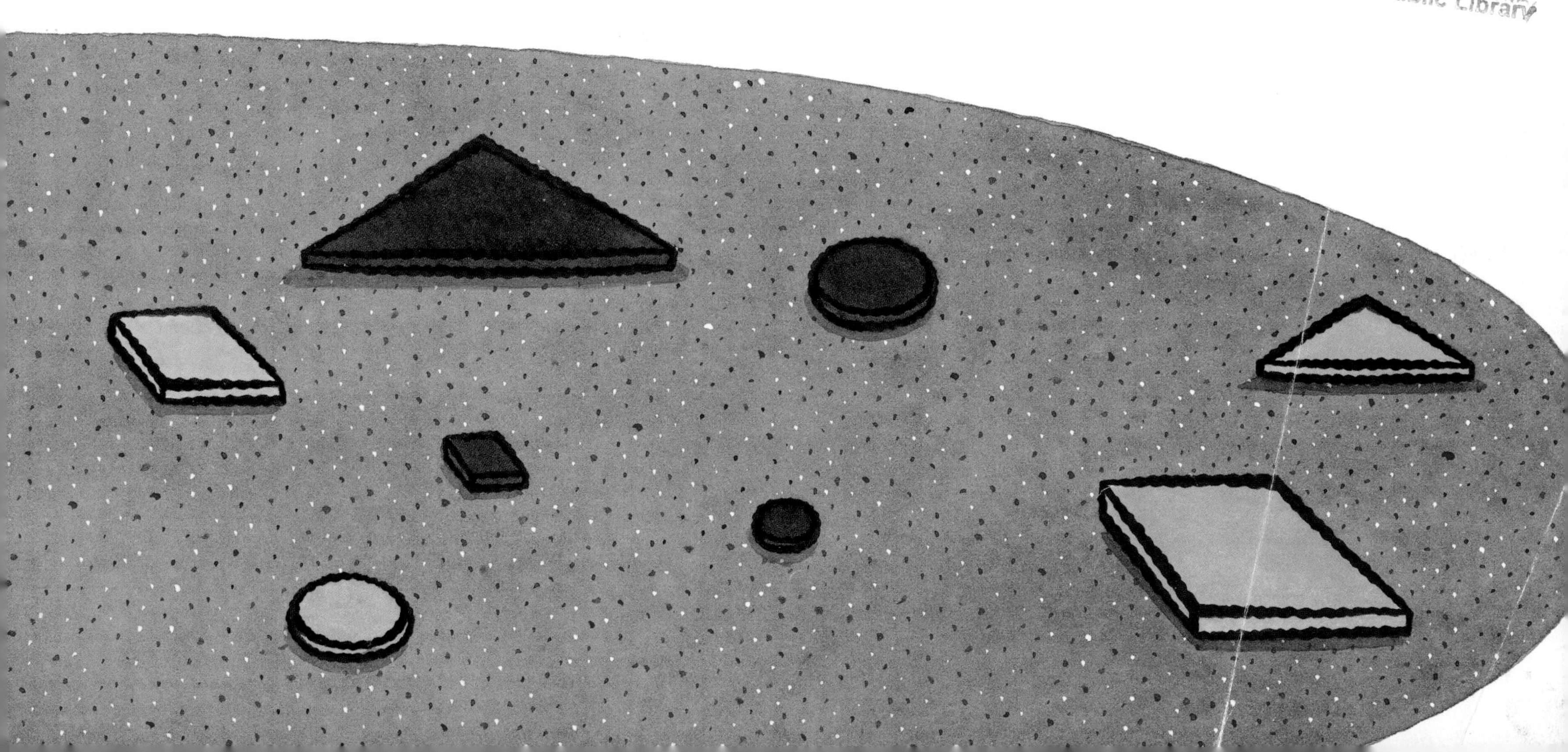

MathStart® SORTING

# 3 Little Firefighters

by Stuart J. Murphy
illustrated by Bernice Lum

HarperCollinsPublishers

*To Charlotte—who is as cute as a button*
*—S.J.M.*

*for "the fledge" and his dog*
*—B.L.*

The publisher and author would like to thank teachers Patricia Chase, Phyllis Goldman, and Patrick Hopfensperger for their help in making the math in MathStart just right for kids.

HarperCollins®, ®, and MathStart® are registered trademarks of HarperCollins Publishers. For more information about the MathStart series, write to HarperCollins Children's Books, 1350 Avenue of the Americas, New York, NY 10019, or visit our website at www.mathstartbooks.com.

Bugs incorporated in the MathStart series design were painted by Jon Buller.

3 Little Firefighters


Library of Congress Cataloging-in-Publication Data
Murphy, Stuart J.
3 Little Firefighters / by Stuart J. Murphy ; illustrated by Bernice Lum.
p. cm. — (MathStart)
"Matching sets."
"Level 1."
Summary: Three young firefighters must find matching sets of buttons to complete their costumes for a parade, but should they sort them by shape, color, or size?
ISBN 0-06-000118-6 — ISBN 0-06-000120-8 (pbk.)
1. Set Theory—Juvenile literature. [1. Set theory.] I. Lum, Bernice, ill. II. Title. III. Series.
QA248 .M77 2003 2002019062
511.3'22—dc21

Typography by Elynn Cohen 2 3 4 5 6 7 8 9 10 ❖ First Edition

# 3 Little Firefighters

We are three little firefighters.
Hurry—let's get dressed!

The parade starts in an hour
and we have to look our best.

But we're missing all our buttons!
We don't know what to do.
Everyone will see our bellies
and our belly buttons, too.

We have to find some buttons,
and the buttons have to match.
Each coat will need four buttons.
We can't have less than that.

We found a bunch of buttons.
But we've got to have four sets.
Let's sort them out by shape,
and find out what we get.

"I found a set of circles!"

But two sets aren't complete.
Our belly buttons will still show
when we're out on the street.

# CLANG, CLANG!

Ink Spot, we have a problem.
This is no time to play.
We've got to get our boots on,
and find buttons right away!

# CLANG, CLANG!

We've really got to hurry.
We have to find three sets.

Let's sort them out by color,
and find out what we get.

"We both have matching buttons!"

"But I don't. I'm afraid
my belly button will still show
when we're in the parade."

WOOOoooOOO!

# WOOOooooOOO!

Ink Spot, don't be silly.
We are not finished yet.

Let's sort the buttons out by size,

and find out what we get.

2
7

Now we each have four buttons,
large, medium, and small.
At last our belly buttons
won't be seen at all.

# WOOF, WOOF!

Ink Spot, no more barking
now that everything is fine.
We'll just sew on our buttons—
"Wait! I'm missing one of mine."

WOOF, WOOF!

Find it! Let's look everywhere!
Turn this place upside down!
Check under the fire truck!

Wait—

Look what Ink Spot has found!

# CLANG, CLANG! Woooo,

# Woooo! Woof, Woof!

Now every button is sewn on.
We're ready on the dot.
We are three little firefighters
with our dog, Ink Spot!

**Woof!**

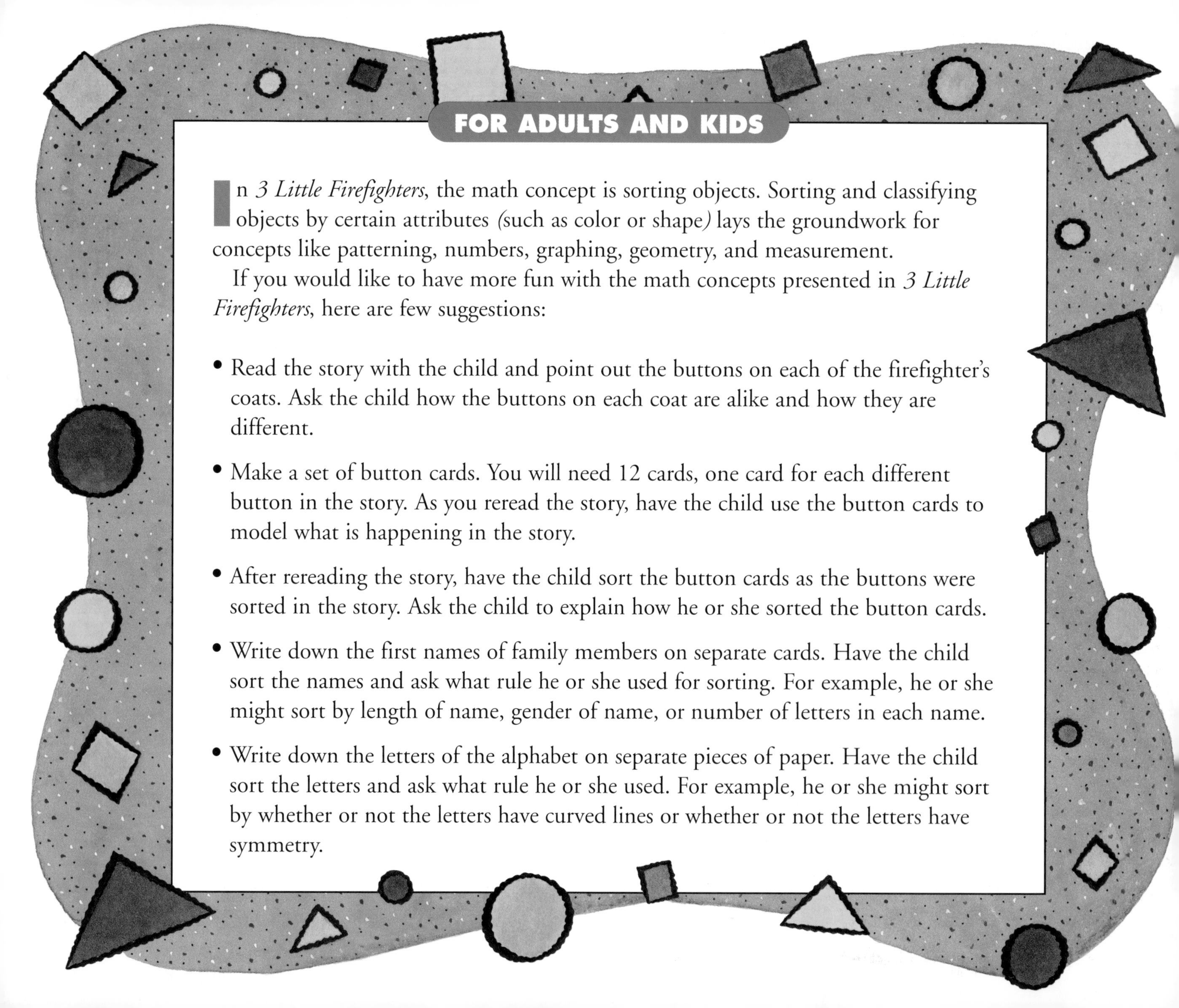

## FOR ADULTS AND KIDS

In *3 Little Firefighters*, the math concept is sorting objects. Sorting and classifying objects by certain attributes (such as color or shape) lays the groundwork for concepts like patterning, numbers, graphing, geometry, and measurement.

If you would like to have more fun with the math concepts presented in *3 Little Firefighters*, here are few suggestions:

- Read the story with the child and point out the buttons on each of the firefighter's coats. Ask the child how the buttons on each coat are alike and how they are different.
- Make a set of button cards. You will need 12 cards, one card for each different button in the story. As you reread the story, have the child use the button cards to model what is happening in the story.
- After rereading the story, have the child sort the button cards as the buttons were sorted in the story. Ask the child to explain how he or she sorted the button cards.
- Write down the first names of family members on separate cards. Have the child sort the names and ask what rule he or she used for sorting. For example, he or she might sort by length of name, gender of name, or number of letters in each name.
- Write down the letters of the alphabet on separate pieces of paper. Have the child sort the letters and ask what rule he or she used. For example, he or she might sort by whether or not the letters have curved lines or whether or not the letters have symmetry.

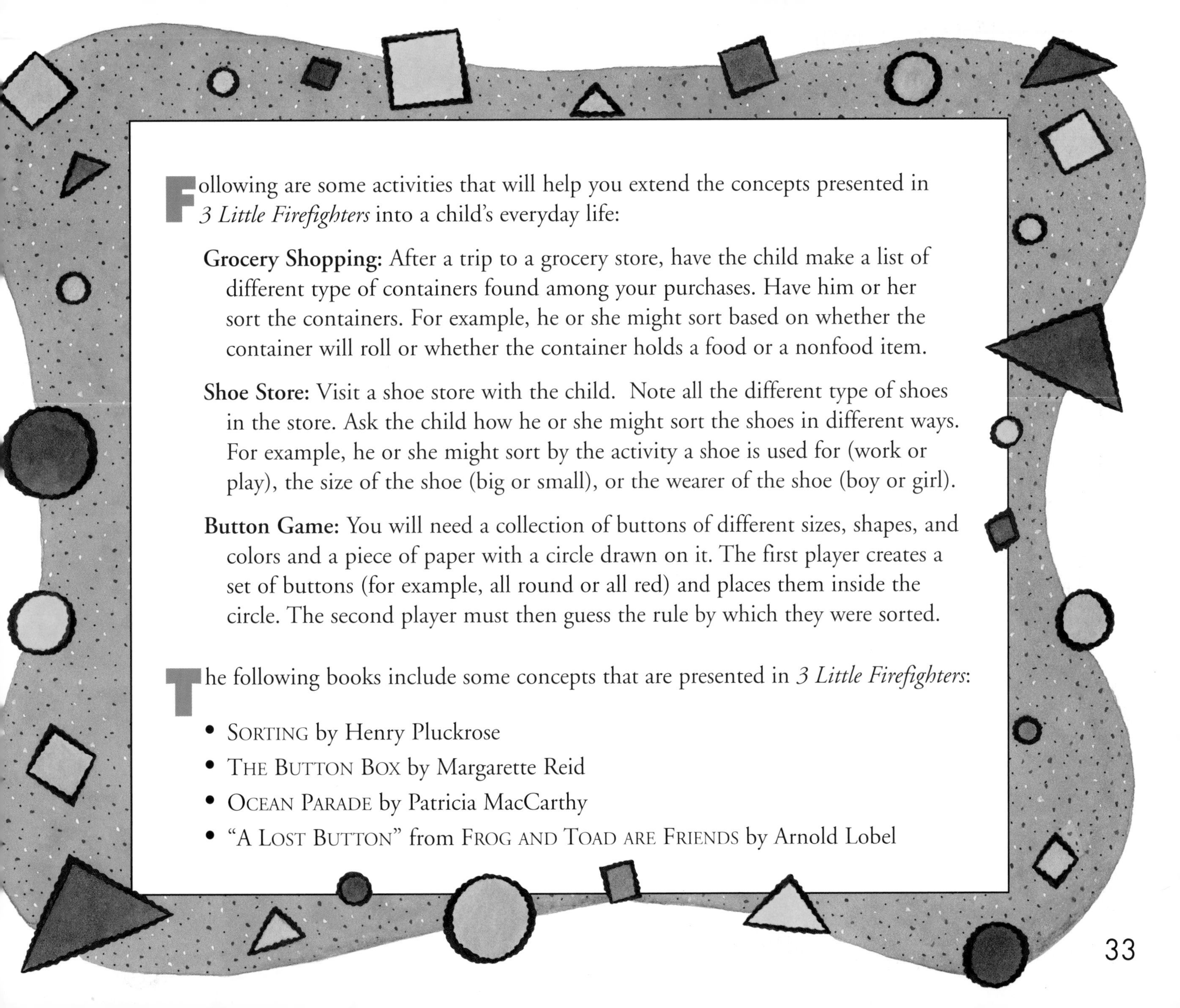

Following are some activities that will help you extend the concepts presented in *3 Little Firefighters* into a child's everyday life:

**Grocery Shopping:** After a trip to a grocery store, have the child make a list of different type of containers found among your purchases. Have him or her sort the containers. For example, he or she might sort based on whether the container will roll or whether the container holds a food or a nonfood item.

**Shoe Store:** Visit a shoe store with the child. Note all the different type of shoes in the store. Ask the child how he or she might sort the shoes in different ways. For example, he or she might sort by the activity a shoe is used for (work or play), the size of the shoe (big or small), or the wearer of the shoe (boy or girl).

**Button Game:** You will need a collection of buttons of different sizes, shapes, and colors and a piece of paper with a circle drawn on it. The first player creates a set of buttons (for example, all round or all red) and places them inside the circle. The second player must then guess the rule by which they were sorted.

The following books include some concepts that are presented in *3 Little Firefighters*:

- SORTING by Henry Pluckrose
- THE BUTTON BOX by Margarette Reid
- OCEAN PARADE by Patricia MacCarthy
- "A LOST BUTTON" from FROG AND TOAD ARE FRIENDS by Arnold Lobel

HLOOX +
E
MURPH



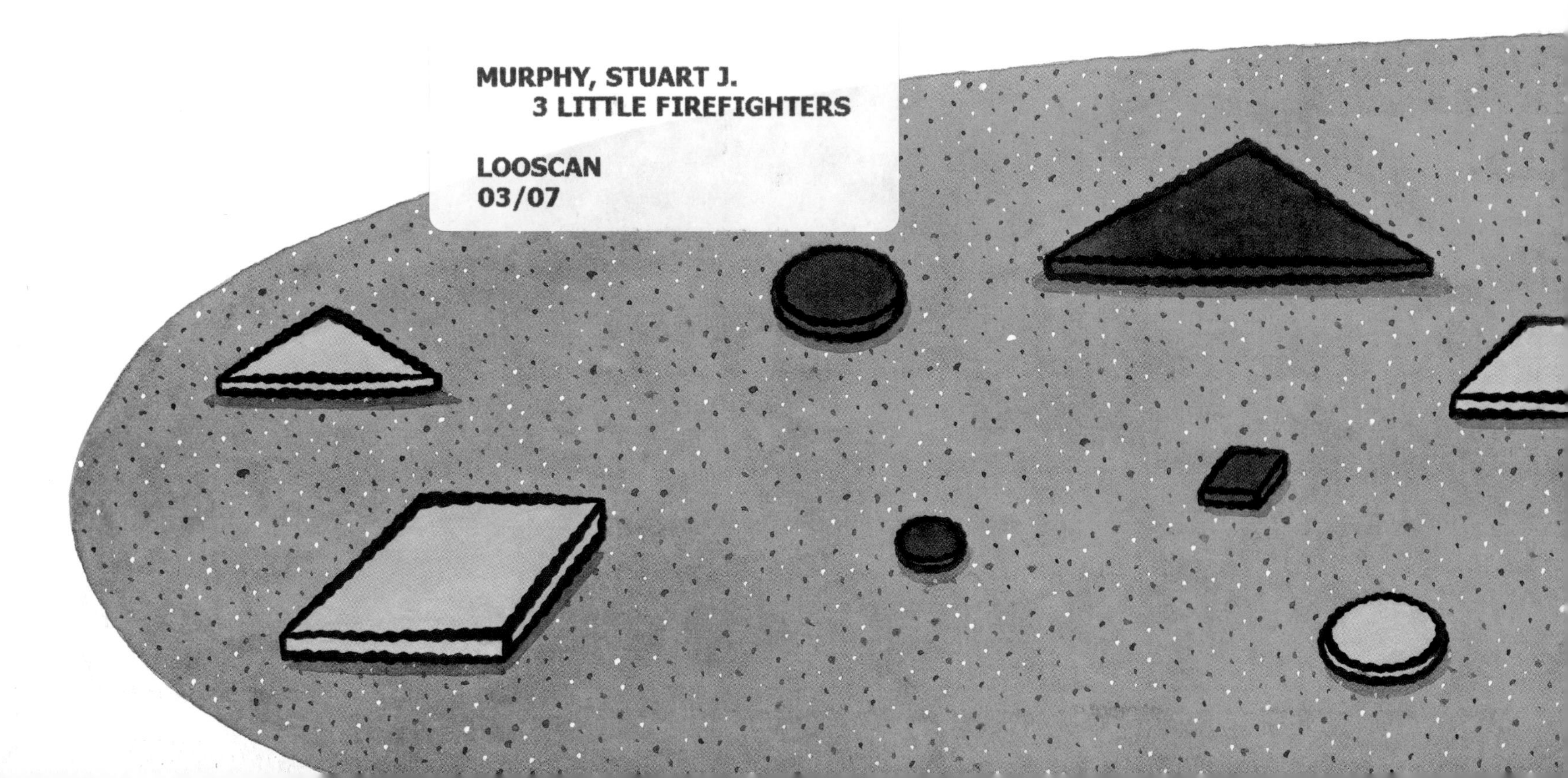